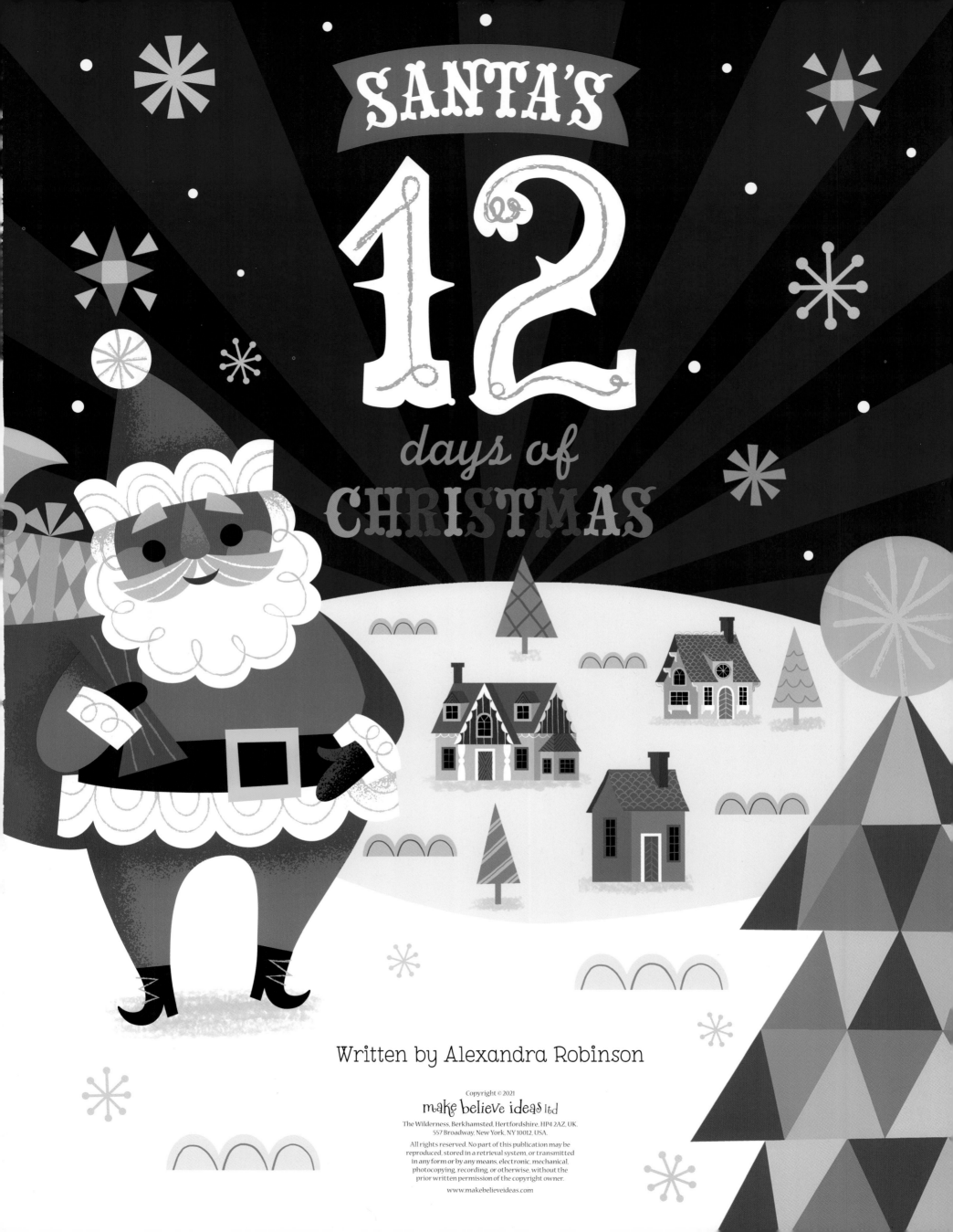

SANTA'S

12

days of
CHRISTMAS

Written by Alexandra Robinson

Copyright © 2021

make believe ideas ltd

The Wilderness, Berkhamsted, Hertfordshire, HP4 2AZ, UK.
557 Broadway, New York, NY 10012, USA.

www.makebelieveideas.com

Have you ever wondered
what **Santa** likes to do
when his deliveries are done,
and *Christmas Eve* is through?

He lands his **sleigh** on *Christmas Day*, greeted by a **cheer**. He's **ready** for a **twelve-day** break— it's been a **busy** year!

On day **1** of the holidays
he throws a **yuletide ball**,
with *disco lights*, red **party hats**,
and **candy canes** for all!

On day **2** Santa takes the **train** through the **sparkling** snow.

JOY

NOEL NOEL 2

He's off to see

The Nutcracker–

his favorite

Christmas show!

On day **3** jolly Mr. C

holds a **reindeer race.**

The **elves** stand by and **watch** with glee

to see who *wins* first place!

On day **4** Santa calls his friends  to *skate* around **outside.**

They *whirl* about across the **lake**
and have **fun** as they **glide**!

On day **5** Santa takes his **wife** to watch the **town parade.**

They **cheer** The **Merry** Marching Band . . .

and praise **The Dance Brigade!**

On day **6** *Santa's* **festive** friends
invite him to the **park,**

where, down the **hill**, they sled and slide

until the **sky** turns **dark!**

On New Year's Eve, the **7th** day,

they all watch with *delight*

as *fireworks* WHIZZ, POP,

and BANG,

filling the **sky** with *light!*

On day **8** Santa takes some **yarn** and *dazzling* glittery **gems**, then settles in his chair to *knit* warm **sweaters** for his friends!

On day **9** Santa and his *pals* enjoy the **frosty** weather.

They play **snow** games,

build **ice** displays,

DAY **9**

and take **photos** together!

On day  Santa plans to try

some **recipes** he's read:

three **cream** tarts,

two *fruit* soufflés,

and a *house* of **gingerbread!**

On day **11** Santa Claus prepares a roaring *fire*, then sings some ***merry carols*** with

The Jolly Jingle Choir!

On day **12** of his *festive* break,
he *polishes* his sleigh.

He's ready to start making plans
for next year's *Christmas Day!*